Disney · PIXAR
FINDING DORY

Adapted by	Illustrated by	Designed by
Amy Novesky	**Satoshi Hashimoto**	**Tony Fejeran**

 A GOLDEN BOOK • NEW YORK

randomhousekids.com

ISBN 978-0-7364-3511-6 (trade) — ISBN 978-0-7364-3512-3 (ebook)

Printed in the United States of America

10 9 8 7 6 5 4 3 2 1

This is
Dory.

**Dory is
forgetful.**

When Dory was young, her parents collected **shells** and made trails for her to follow so she would always find her way home.

One day, Dory spotted a pretty **purple shell**
in the distance. She wasn't allowed
to swim that far. But Dory forgot.

Dory was just about to
pick up the shell when—

wHOOSH!

—she was pulled
away by the undertow.

Suddenly, Dory was **all alone**.

She **couldn't** find her way home.

Eventually, she forgot what she was looking for. No one was able to help.

And then she crashed into **Marlin**. Marlin was far from home, too. He was looking for his son, Nemo.

A h h hhh!

Dory helped Marlin cross the ocean and find Nemo. She went to live with them in the coral reef. She finally had a new **home**.

One day, Dory went with Nemo's class on a field trip to see the **stingray migration**. Dory got pulled into the undertow!

When Dory returned to safety, she was
flooded with **memories** of her mom and dad.

She **remembered** where she was
from! Dory wanted to go home.

With the help of some old friends, Marlin and Nemo joined Dory on her trip across the ocean . . .

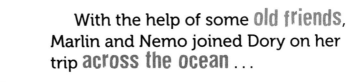

. . . all the way to Morro Bay, where she was scooped up and

taken
away!

Dory found herself in a tank
inside the Marine Life Institute.
This was where she was from.

A **cranky** septopus—
a seven-armed octopus—
named **Hank** greeted Dory
and agreed to help her
find her family.

He had three hearts,
after all.

But Dory was tossed into the Whale Shark pool, which is where Dory met Destiny.

When Destiny heard Dory speak Whale, she couldn't believe it.

"Dory, is that you?"

When Dory lived at the Marine Life Institute, Dory and Destiny had been **pipe pals**! They used to talk through the pipes that connected their tanks.

Destiny knew where Dory had grown up!

"Your Whale has gotten really good," Destiny said.

"Thaaannnk yoouu!"

Hank soon joined them. Dory told Destiny and her neighbor, **Bailey**, a beluga whale, that she was looking for her family.

Destiny told Dory to take the pipes to the **Open Ocean exhibit**. That was where she would find her family.

Dory was worried she would get lost in the pipes, so she found another way.

Hank and Dory
rolled...

...**swam**...

. . . and **swung** across the Institute to the Open Ocean exhibit.

Dory was sad to say **goodbye** to Hank. She would miss him. But he wanted to go to Cleveland. "You'll forget me in a heartbeat. Three heartbeats. Now go find your family," said Hank.

Dory asked around for help, but no one knew where her family was. Then she saw something.

Dory found her house! But it was **empty**.
Suddenly, Dory was filled with memories. She remembered her mom and dad hugging her. She had to find them!
Dory spotted a **purple shell** in the distance.

As she swam toward it, she met a **crab** who told her if she went through the pipes, she would find her parents.

She followed the directions and ended up in the ocean!

She was all alone again.

Dory worried that she'd never find her way home. Then she spotted another shell, and another.

Dory followed
a trail of
s h e l l s...

. . . and she found her
mom and **dad**!

Dory was home again, surrounded by her **family** and all of her friends.